KERMIT'S DOUBLE TROUBLE

Adapted by Kirsten Mayer

Based on the screenplay by James Bobin & Nicholas Stoller

Illustrated by Artful Doodlers

LITTLE, BROWN AND COMPANY
New York   Boston

Little, Brown and Company

Hachette Book Group
237 Park Avenue, New York, NY 10017
Visit our website at lb-kids.com

Little, Brown and Company is a division of Hachette Book Group, Inc.
The Little, Brown name and logo are trademarks of Hachette Book Group, Inc.

The publisher is not responsible for websites (or their content) that are not owned by the publisher.

First Edition: February 2014

ISBN 978-0-316-27763-1

Library of Congress Control Number: 2013945110

10 9 8 7 6 5 4 3 2 1

CW

Printed in the United States of America

Meanwhile…
The Muppets are on a world tour!
The gang has taken the show on the road,
and the first stop is in Berlin, Germany.

THE MUPPETS

GESUCHT!

EVILEN FROGGEN

1000,-

"Okay, guys," Kermit tells the Muppets, "let's perform what we know! We'll open with the cabaret number, then Fozzie's jokes, then Piggy's song, and then..."

Gonzo raises his hand. "Kermit, when do I get to perform my indoor Running of the Bulls stunt?"

Miss Piggy bats her eyelashes. "Kermie, I want to sing *five* songs."

"Guys!" shouts Kermit. "We can't just do whatever we want. This is opening night of the entire tour—it has to go well! Let's just play to our strengths."

Miss Piggy follows Kermit back to his dressing room.

"Kermie, let's talk about our wedding. I have swatches for the seat covers...."

"What? How can we get married when I haven't even asked you to marry me yet?" protests Kermit.

"You never let me do what I want!" huffs Miss Piggy, and she storms angrily out of the room.

Kermit feels bad. He knows someone has to keep the show running smoothly, but it is a hard job sometimes. He goes for a quiet stroll along the river to clear his head.

He is gone for a while....

After the show in Berlin, the Muppets
head to the next stop on their tour: Madrid,
Spain.

THE MUPPETS

"What will we do in the show tonight, boss?" asks Scooter.

"I don't care," answers the frog. "Do whatever you want."

Gonzo pleads, "Can I do the indoor Running of the Bulls?"

"Say, what's wrong with your voice, anyway?" asks Scooter, noticing Kermit's voice has sounded different ever since they left Berlin.

"Kermie, if he can do his thing, can I sing five songs?" adds Miss Piggy.

The frog waves a hand. "Sure, Zongo, go ahead. And yes, Pig, why not?"

The Muppets cheer and run off to prepare to do whatever they want in the show!

It seems as if Kermit has had a
change of heart, so Miss Piggy follows
him again to talk.

"Kermie?" she starts.
The frog turns to her. "Ah, Miss Pig. Ah yes, I am your man, and you are my
lady. Stick with me, as we are meant to be together forever."
"Oh, Kermie!" she cries, blushing.

With Kermit's new attitude, everyone does what they want during the show, and it lasts three hours!

The next stop on the Muppets world tour is Dublin, Ireland.

THE MUPPETS

Before the show, Fozzie shows an Irish newspaper to Animal and Walter. "Hey," the bear says, "why is Kermit on the front page?"

Walter looks and says, "That's not Kermit. See that big mole on his face? That's Constantine, the World's Most Dangerous Frog!"

Animal shouts, "BAD FROG! BAD FROG!"

Walter gasps. "Wait…Kermit has been acting strangely lately. What if Kermit has been replaced by this Constantine guy?" he asks.

The three friends go to Kermit's dressing room and look around. Walter finds a pot of green makeup on the desk.

"He must put this makeup over his mole to hide it!" he says.

"AAAAAH!" shouts Fozzie. "Why is he here? Where's Kermit?"

"They must have somehow switched places, and Kermit must be the frog they put in prison," says Walter. "Come on, guys. We've got to go find the real Kermit!"

Walter, Fozzie, and Animal set out to find Kermit.

Meanwhile, the other Muppets have been doing whatever they want, but they wonder if whatever they want is what they really want.

"Maybe it's just me," says Gonzo, "but is doing whatever we want not as fun as we thought it would be?"

Rowlf nods. "You know when you're a kid and you want a cool dad and then you hang out with your friend's cool dad and it is weird and then you miss your normal dad who made all the rules?" he asks.

"Yeah," says Scooter. "Does anyone else feel like maybe Kermit's acting differently on this tour?"

Miss Piggy snorts. "I don't know what you're talking about. Kermie has never paid more attention to me."

"That's kind of our point," says Scooter.

That night, at the show in Dublin, the frog interrupts Miss Piggy's sixth musical number with a big surprise.

"Miss Piggy, I want to ask you a very important question. Do you wish to marry me and become Mrs. the Frog?"

"Oh, Kermie, yes!" she squeals.

The frog turns to the audience and announces, "We will be married in two days' time at the Tower of London!"

Miss Piggy is happy, but she finally wonders if Kermit is acting weirdly.
"This doesn't feel right—it's too easy," Piggy says to her dog, Foo-Foo.
"Love shouldn't be easy."

Two days later, Miss Piggy is at the Tower of London in a beautiful dress, standing with the frog she agreed to marry.

Miss Piggy isn't sure what to do. Something doesn't feel right....

Then Kermit suddenly drops in, right next to the false frog! Animal, Walter, and Fozzie found their friend and made it to the wedding just in time!

Miss Piggy gets angry. "Two Kermits?!" she cries. "How can there be *two Kermits*?"

The real Kermit chimes in, "That's not me! I'm me! He's Constantine, the World's Most Dangerous Frog!"

"He's lying! I'm the real Kermit," says Constantine.

This back-and-forth goes on for a while.

Finally Piggy says, "I know how to settle this. First Kermit, will you marry me?"

"Yes, of course, there is a helicopter waiting...."

"Second Kermit, will you marry me?"

"Um, well, I'm not...it's just..." stutters Kermit.

"THAT'S my Kermie!" Piggy cries, and she hugs her frog.

The criminal finally wipes the makeup off his mole and reveals himself to the crowd.

"I paid audiences to come to the shows! I robbed museums right next door while you were performing! Then I set you up to take the blame! In fact, this wedding is a cover-up for my greatest heist yet: stealing the Crown Jewels of England next door! So long, suckers!"

And with that, Constantine runs and hops aboard a getaway helicopter.

But the Muppets aren't about to let him get away. Kermit runs and grabs hold of the helicopter, and Gonzo onto him, and Fozzie onto him, and Walter onto him…and so on. The Muppet chain finally stops Constantine from getting away!

Sam Eagle handcuffs the criminal mastermind, Constantine. "Did you
know this frog robbed museums in Berlin, Madrid, Dublin, and London?" he
asks the Muppets.

"All those sound familiar," Walter says, nodding.

"And you caught him!" says Sam. "Congratulations, weirdos."

Kermit turns to Miss Piggy. "Sorry I ruined your wedding."
"Oh, Kermie, I'm so glad you did," sighs Miss Piggy.

The end!

GRAND TOUR

MAR	FRI 24	BERLIN	DAS LOCH IN DER WAND VEREIN	800-555-0199
	SAT 25	DUSSELDORF	THEATER GUTEN ZEITEN	800-656-1482
	SUN 26	HAMBURG	GERNE THEATER BAYERN	800-654-2192
	MON 27	MUDBURG	KASE UND WAFFELN THEATER	888-374-6483
	TUE 28	VOMITDORF	THEATER ROTEN LOWEN GRUNEN ELEFANTEN	888-728-6483
	WED 29	POOPENBURGEN	ORT DER TRAUME THEATER	877-504-8423
APR	FRI 01	BRUCKANDERMUR	WORGL THEATER	800-656-1482
	SAT 02	KLOSTERNEUBERG	BISHOFSHOFEN UND WAFFELN THEATER	888-374-6483
	MON 03	SANKTJOHANNIM	THEATER MURZZUSCHLAG	800-654-2192
	TUE 04	MEDAYESEGYHAZA	THEATER MASONMAGYAROVAR	877-504-8423
	WED 05	HODMEZOVASARHELY	KISKUNFELEGYHAZA	800-555-0199
	THU 06	PARIS	LE KREMLIN-BICETRE	800-654-2192
	FRI 07	VILLENEUVE-LA-GARENNE	COUDEKERQUE-BRANCHE	888-374-6483
	SAT 08	SAINT-MENARD-EN-JALLES	THEATER BLAGNAC	800-656-1482
	MON 09	NOISY-LE-GRAND	PETIT BOURG	877-504-8423
	TUE 10	LONDON	WEST END REVUE THEATRE	800-656-1482
	WED 11	BROADBOTTOM	LITTLE WEEDON THEATRE	888-374-6483
	THU 12	UPPER PIDDLE	LONELY BACHELORS THEATRE	888-374-6483
	FRI 13	DUBLIN	GARRANGIBBON THEATRE	800-555-0199
	SAT 14	CHEESEMOUNT	CARRICK ON SUIR MUNSTER	800-656-1482

R. Harris